Raindrop
Bill

First published in 2008 by
Franklin Watts
338 Euston Road
London
NW1 3BH

Franklin Watts Australia
Level 17/207 Kent Street
Sydney
NSW 2000

A CIP catalogue record for this book is available
from the British Library.

ISBN 978 0 7496 7941 5 (hbk)
ISBN 978 0 7496 7953 8 (pbk)

Series Editor: Jackie Hamley
Series Advisor: Dr Barrie Wade
Series Designer: Peter Scoulding

Printed in China

Franklin Watts is a division of
Hachette Children's Books,
an Hachette Livre UK company.

For lovely, lovely Martin –
the best son-in-law in the world!
– A.B.

Raindrop Bill

by Ann Bryant

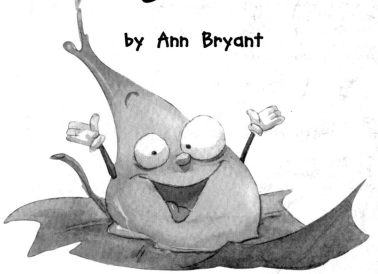

Illustrated by O'Kif

W

FRANKLIN WATTS

LONDON・SYDNEY

A raindrop fell down
from a cloud.

His name was
Raindrop Bill.

He fell and fell ...

and fell and fell ...

... then plopped onto a hill.

Next he rolled ...

and rolled ...

and rolled ...

... and slipped into
a stream.

He floated on his back
and sang out,

"Life is just a dream!"

He entertained the fishes
with his little raindrop song.

But then the stream
began to race,
and Bill got
swept along.

15

He rushed into a river
as a leaf fell from a tree.

And Bill cried,
"Look I'm sailing!"

Then he sailed right out to sea!

Poor little Raindrop Bill
got scared.

He wished that he could hide.

But suddenly the Air took
Raindrop Bill up for a ride.

It scooped him up
and up ... and up ...

... and sat him on a cloud.

And Bill was one of many,
many raindrops in a crowd.

He felt himself grow heavy,

and he slipped and slid
and then ...

He tumbled from the cloud
and called out,

Leapfrog Rhyme Time has been specially designed to fit the requirements of the Literacy Framework. It offers real books for beginner readers by top authors and illustrators. There are 27 Leapfrog Rhyme Time stories to choose from: